295

hal

D1349450

For Dad, and all those who share his
sense of humour.

First published in Great Britain in 2005 by Bloomsbury Publishing Plc
38 Soho Square, London, W1D 3HB

Copyright © Adrian Johnson 2005
The moral right of the author and illustrator has been asserted

A CIP catalogue record of this book is available from the British Library

ISBN 0 7475 7431 6

All papers used by Bloomsbury Publishing are natural, recyclable
products made from wood grown in well-managed forests. The
manufacturing processes conform to the environmental regulations of
the country of origin.

Printed in China by South China Printing Co

1 3 5 7 9 10 8 6 4 2

that's NOT funny!

ADRIAN JOHNSON

BLOOMSBURY
CHILDREN'S
BOOKS

ALFIE LIKES TO LAUGH*

...HA HA HAHAHAHA HA HA HA HA HAHAHA!
HAHAHA HAHA **HAHAHAHA** HA HAHAHA HAHAHAHA !
HA HAHA ha ha ha ha HA HAHAHAHA!
HA! HA! HA! HAHA chaha HAHAHA HAHAHA!!!

(*in particular, he likes to laugh at other people's misfortune)

Mr Swiss →

Alfie laughs at his grandpa all the time.

salt sugar

One Saturday when Grandpa said,

Fancy going into town?

Alfie said,

OH, YES!

There'd be a lot of things to laugh at in town.

On the way to the station, Alfie chuckled when a
mean-looking dog chased the postman down the street.

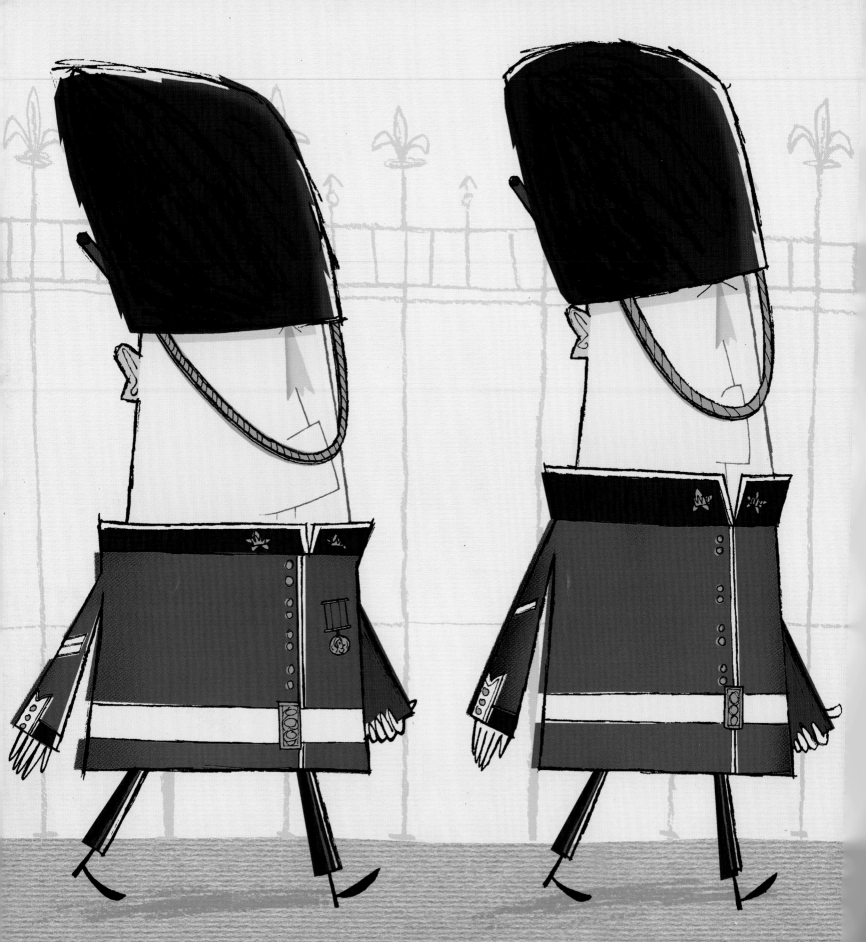

Outside the Palace he giggled when one of the guards ...

... tripped over Mr Swiss.

In the park he laughed a rackety laugh
when a jogger jogged ...

Outside the department store he cackled gleefully when a window cleaner accidentally soaked a tourist.

'What a funny day!' said Alfie.
'Well, I can't see what you find so funny,' said Grandpa.
On the way home Grandpa had an idea.

'LET'S GO TO THE CIRCUS!' Grandpa said.
'Now THAT will be funny.'

But Alfie wasn't so sure.

He sulked all the way to **BARRY MANCHEGO'S BIG TOP OF BIG CHEESE.**

Alfie watched the acrobats, but there wasn't even a sign of a giggle, a cackle, or a chuckle out of him.

But Mr Swiss had his eye on something else.

HOLY EMMENTHAL! IT'S THE WORLD'S LARGEST CHEESE!

Before Alfie could stop him, Mr Swiss had vanished.

Mr Swiss raced across the Big Top ...

... and past Oberon the elephan

COME BACK, MR SWISS!

Oberon jumped so high he nearly hit the roof.

Then Oberon began to DROP ...

... RIGHT on to Alfie!

The audience saw the whole thing.
There was a giggle,
a cackle,
and a chuckle.
And they all exploded into laughter.

THAT'S NOT FUNNY!!!

said Alfie.

But actually it was – wouldn't you agree?

SCHADENFREUDE
SCHADENFREUDE
SCHADENFREUDE
SCHADENFREUDE
SCHADENFREUDE

means 'a malicious delight in the bad luck of others'.

schardenfrood?

schredenfeeder?

schrarden-frudy?

schadenfreude!

We don't have an English word
for **schadenfreude**, so we thought
it would be a good idea to borrow
this word from the German.
It's pronounced 'shardenfroyder'.
Why don't you try saying it yourself?